BABAR™

BABAR SAILS AWAY

Written by Lesley Young
With illustrations by Ley Honor Roberts

MADCAP

Happy Birthday Pom!
Happy Birthday Flora!
Happy Birthday Alexander!
The little elephants slide down the banister.

Celeste brings in some toast with smiling faces on it.

'What are we going to do today?' ask the children.

'Are we going to the cinema?' asks Flora.

'Is it a trip to the theatre?' asks Alexander.

'I know,' says Pom, grabbing the corner of the tablecloth, ready to whisk it off, 'We're going to have a conjuror!'

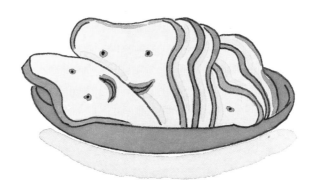

'No. We're going to do something much more exciting,' says Babar.

He has cut up a banana and put it on his toast, like tusks.

'We're going up, up and away in your hot air balloon,' shouts Alexander, leaping up.

'No, we're going to have a picnic,' says Babar.

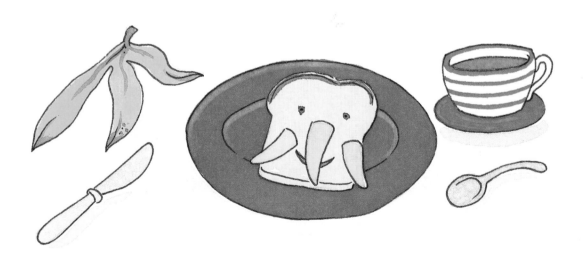

'A picnic?' The children don't seem very excited.
'But not just any old picnic,' says Babar.
'Wait and see.'
'Come on,' says Celeste, 'and help me fill the
hamper.'
Flora puts in iced buns. Alexander
puts in crisps. Pom adds ginger beer.
'Happy Birthday! Wait for me!' shouts
Arthur, running in with a bunch
of balloons

They bundle into Babar's car and drive off to a park.

'Let's set out the picnic beside this hedge,' says Babar.

'Hedges are boring,' says Pom. 'Can't we have it beside the lake? Or the swings?'

'This is a special hedge,' says Arthur. 'Look – there's a door in it, and a sign saying "This Way".

'It's a maze,' says Babar, 'and when we've eaten we'll explore it. But we must all stick together.'

'Arthur,' says Celeste, 'why are you eating so quickly? There's no rush.'

'That's what you think!' says Arthur, throwing up a bun with his trunk and catching it in his mouth.

Arthur gets up and runs into the maze. The three children run after him and disappear inside.

'Well, they're in a hurry,' laughs Babar.

Celeste begins to laugh as well and says to him, 'They'll find their way out, I'm sure.'

But time passes and the children don't appear. Celeste stands on the picnic hamper and peers over the hedge. All she sees is more hedges.

Babar reaches for one of the birthday balloons and bounces it on the grass.

'I'm getting a little worried,' says Celeste.

'This balloon has given me an idea,' says Babar, as the balloon floats up in the sky. 'Wait here.'

Babar rushes back to the palace. 'Quick – help me blow up my hot air balloon!' he says. Elephants from all sides rush over to help. Zephir darts around, getting in the way.

Celeste is amazed to see Babar and Zephir sailing towards her, waving from the balloon basket.

'Hop in – we'll soon find the children.' Celeste climbs in and they float over the edge of the maze.

The Balloon sails over the hedges until it reaches the middle of the maze.

'There they are!' Pom and Arthur are lifting Flora so that she can see over the hedge. Babar lets down a rope ladder and Zephir scurries down and helps them all up into the basket.

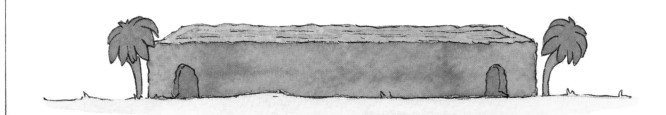

'So we had a balloon trip after all,' laughs Flora
as they all sail away over the tree tops. 'This must be
our best birthday ever.'

This work conceived, produced and originally published in 1999 by Madcap Books,
André Deutsch Ltd, 76 Dean Street, London, W1V 5HA www.vci.co.uk

Babar characters™ and © 1999 Laurent de Brunhoff. Licensed by Nelvana Limited and The Clifford Ross Company Ltd.

Adapted by Lesley Young and Ley Honor Roberts, and based on characters created by Jean and Laurent de Brunhoff.

Design by David Butler. Reprographics by Digicol Link

A catalogue record for this title is available from the British Library

ISBN 0 233 99520 X

Printed in Italy by Officine Grafiche DeAgostini